DEAR YOUNG READER,

CONGRATULATIONS! YOU ARE ABOUT TO EXPLORE ALBEE'S OCEAN WORLD. ALBEE WAS AN ALBINO THRESHER SHARK AND HIS HOME WAS AROUND THE CLEAR BLUE WATER OF MALAPASCUA (MALAPAS-KWA) ISLAND.

YOUR JOURNEY WITH ALBEE WILL HELP YOU UNDERSTAND THAT BULLYING AND TEASING CAN REALLY HURT SOMEONE'S FEELINGS.

ALBEE WILL TEACH YOU HOW WE CAN PROTECT OUR BEAUTIFUL OCEAN AND THE SEA CREATURES LIVING IN IT SO THAT WE ALL CAN ENJOY ITS' BEAUTY AND BOUNTY.

WANT TO BE HAPPY? ALBEE REVEALED THE SECRET OF LASTING HAPPINESS.

WANT TO LEARN SOME NEW WORDS AND IDEAS? ALBEE ENCOURAGED YOU TO CHECK ANY NEW WORDS IN THE DICTIONARY AND/OR ASK THE HELP OF YOUR FAMILY MEMBERS OR EVEN A FRIEND!

THANK YOU FOR YOUR READING INTEREST AND I HOPE ALBEE COULD HELP EXPAND YOUR WORLD.

SINCERELY,

EDNA DURAN
(AUTHOR – ALBEE, A THRESHER SHARK, 2015)

ALBEE

A THRESHER SHARK

BY EDNA DURAN

Illustrations by Hope Valiente

the Peppertree Press

Sarasota, Florida

ACKNOWLEDGEMENTS

I am truly grateful to….
* Michael Keith Modina - Info coordinator for Malapascua, thresher shark and seaweed noodles.
* Hope Valiente - Very talented digital artist: imaginer and Illustrator
* John Duran - Malapascua dive inspired me to create Albee's story
* Marivic Otero - Info coordinator for toblee plant
* Corazon (Mom) - Gift of literary talent
* Talented team of Peppertree Press: Julie Ann Howell, Teri Lynn Franco and Becky Barbier

YOU ALL MADE THIS BOOK POSSIBLE - THANK YOU VERY MUCH! – Edna Duran

DEDICATION

To the most important men in my life:
My husband Paul and our two sons, John and Leo,
who achieved professional success beyond our expectation.
Love you!

For information regarding permission,
call 941-922-2662 or contact us at our website:
www.peppertreepublishing.com or write to:
the Peppertree Press, LLC.
Attention: Publisher
1269 First Street, Suite 7
Sarasota, Florida 34236

ISBN: 978-1-61493-337-3
Library of Congress Number: 2014921668
Printed March 2015

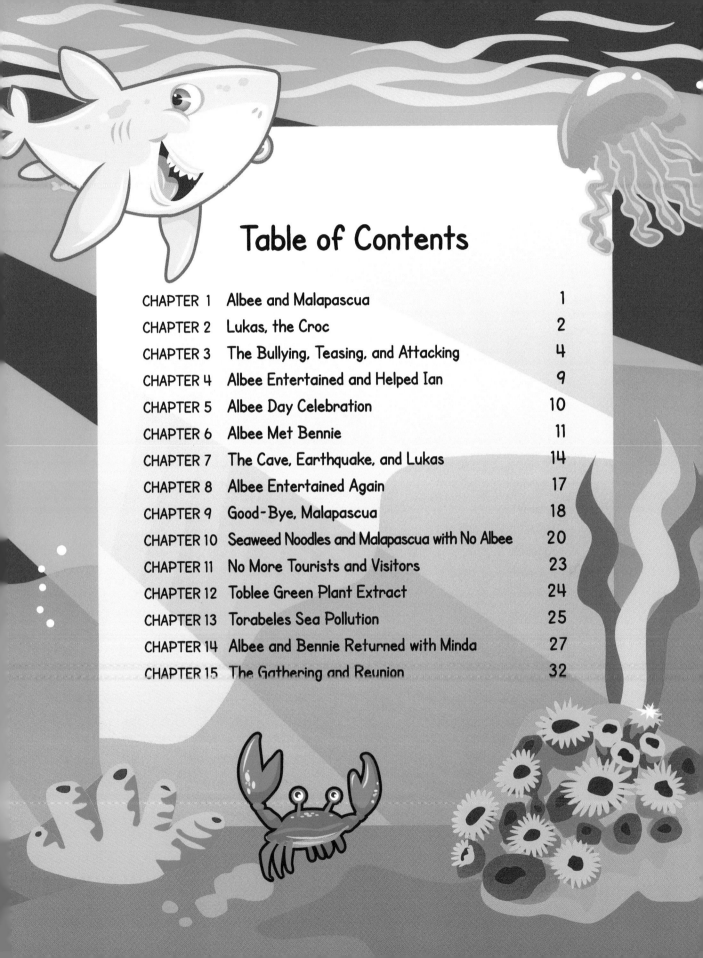

Table of Contents

CHAPTER ONE

Albee and Malapascua

There was once a young thresher shark that lived in the clear blue water of Malapascua, a small island located in the northern Pacific Ocean. His name was Albee and he was albino. His color was creamy, instead of blue-gray like his mommy and daddy. Albee's different look never bothered his parents. Instead, they loved him more and were even proud of him.

But thresher sharks his age and larger sea creatures thought Albee looked odd and weird. They bullied, teased, and even tried to hurt him. Nobody wanted to make friends with him and it made Albee sad.

For humans, however, Albee's different look made him quite popular with boys and girls, moms and dads, including grandmas and grandpas. They were so fond of Albee, even little babies showed fondness for Albee but in a different way.

A mom named Tammy placed a plush toy Albee in front of her little baby girl, Kitty. With stretched arms, Kitty flipped and flapped, then grabbed Albee by his fin. She brought the toy near her mouth, then licked and kissed his cute snout!

The island residents adored and loved Albee. His presence in Malapascua turned a sleepy island into a tourist destination all year round.

One beautiful summer day, while waiting for the boat operator to call passengers for an Albee Sighting Trip, moms and dads, boys and girls, young ladies and guys, and grandmas and grandpas spent the remaining minutes viewing a life-sized photo of Albee in a hotel lobby curiously named, "HOTEL ALBEE."

"Gail, Gail!" called out a little boy to his older sister who was coming down the stairs. "Come quickly and look at Albee's tail! It's very long and wavy like the kite given to me by Uncle Harvey!"

"That's right Danny. It's as long his body. What a cutie!" Gail amusingly agreed as she edged herself closer to her brother.

"Wow! Albee's skin reminds me of a vanilla ice cream I loved to eat in Italy, very nice and creamy!" said a joyful grandma from Sydney, Australia.

"And look at those baseball-size big eyes!" chimed a male Vietnamese tourist, somewhat amazed and amused.

"With those eyes, he can easily catch prey. It must be scary to be the prey." said a dad carrying his two-year-old son who kept pointing at Albee's big eyes, then touched his own eyes and did it all over again.

"Dad, you are silly, thresher sharks do not eat or bite humans. They are gentle sharks, but if you are not careful, they can easily slap you with their wavy tails!" cautioned a teen-aged boy to his dad.

"Thanks for that good information, son."

"I heard threshers can leap out of the water and they prefer to hunt food at night or early morning...and use their tail to stun fish," said a young male visitor from nearby town.

"Well, what are we waiting for? Let's go and see Albee now!" said the joyful grandma from Sydney, Australia.

"All aboard, all aboard!" yelled the boat operator.

Happily they sailed to the open sea, hoping to have a glimpse of the popular albino thresher shark that everyone was excited to see!

CHAPTER TWO

Lukas, the Croc

The story about Albee's popularity was passed on from sea creature to sea creature and soon it reached Lukas, an eight-foot male albino sea crocodile. He lived in Pilar Island, a far-away island north of Malapascua. The news about Albee did not set well for Lukas and he planned to move to Malapascua Island, so that he would, once again, become popular with humans—or so he thought.

Perched at the edge of a sandbar, a very mad Lukas made a loud grunting sound and roared. Then he brazenly yelled, "I AM THE KING OF THE OCEAN AND THERE SHOULD BE NO OTHER KING BUT ME!!" Sea creatures nearby heard Lukas yell, so they all swam away scared. They hid under rocks and reefs, then waited there until Lukas disappeared.

Lukas, the Croc

Humans and sea creatures in Pilar Island knew Lukas to be a hideous, menacing, easily jealous, and gullible crocodile.

No sea creatures wished to be his friend and humans worked hard to get rid of him. They tried…and tried to move him to very far places again and again. Somehow, Lukas always came back with a grunt and a grin!

One day while swimming towards the edge of a small island complaining to no one but himself he said, "I know now why moms and dads, boys and girls, and grandmas and grandpas no longer come to see me! It must be because of this white shark!! I am jealous…he stole the attention away from me and I need to check him out."

Lukas swam across wide body of water and finally arrived in Malapascua in the middle of the night. He hid under the white sand, showing only part of his snout and eyes.

"This is perfect…this is where I will wait for Albee and then attack him!"

He waited…and waited, but Albee did not show up for him. So he swam to the surface and spotted a boatload of tourists. He smiled and showed his dirty rugged teeth, but the tourists were not impressed.

"Go away, you croc with ugly teeth, you are scaring the kids and us!" yelled a papa tourist. Lukas hissed and became upset. He tried to ram the catamaran, but gave up when he saw the captain aim his gun. Lukas swam back to the sand promising to revenge humans.

3

The Bullying, Teasing, and Attacking

It was a sunny mid-afternoon and high tide was about to happen in Malapascua. Albee, his mom Sofia, and his dad Apo followed the movement of fish that went with the tide so that they could have something to eat.

"Oh I love these waves…up and down I go! I wish I could swim on my own without my mom and dad nearby, but I am too scared of those bully sharks and fish!" Albee thought.

A white-bellied eagle was flying above Albee. He yelled, "Hey, white shark, stay close to your mom and dad and be careful, because there is a white crocodile looking for you…just trying to warn you!"

"What do you mean, Mr. Eagle?"

"Well, I heard from fish, sharks, and other birds that crocodile Lukas is jealous because you are popular with humans…he might harm you."

"Who is Lukas?"

"Lukas is a white crocodile who lived around an island farther from here, but decided to move where you live. He became mad and jealous when he heard that you are more popular than him and he is quite mean."

"Thank you, Mr. Eagle, for warning me." Albee looked right, left, below him, and towards his tail. "Okay, I'm safe…no Lukas the croc." Then he called his parents who were a short distance from him.

"Mom and Dad, please don't swim too fast...I'm scared!"

Apo and Sonia turned around and swam toward Albee.

"What's the matter, son?" asked Apo.

"Mr. Eagle warned me of a white crocodile named Lukas who is jealous of me. He wants to hurt me. I am already hated by two thresher sharks, Rico and Max, and now there's a third one—a mean croc!"

"Son, please think of yourself as better and smarter than Lukas, Max, and Rico. Show them that you are brave and strong. You were born with eyes bigger than that of other threshers and if you see danger, swim away quickly!" said Sonia. Apo nodded in agreement.

"Okay, Mom and Dad, I will try to remember what you just said." Then they continued with their 'fish hunting.'

Suddenly, Albee noticed a large field of sea grass below him with colony upon colony of pink shrimp swimming between the stalks. He asked, "Mom and Dad, could you please come down with me below so that I can have some shrimp to eat? I love pink shrimp!"

"Albee, you are now older and, therefore, you no longer need our company. You can swim down yourself, son," said Sonia.

"But Mom ...there might be some big sharks and big fish bullies and maybe Lukas, the white crocodile, lurking behind those tall grass and I'm afraid of them!"

Apo whispered to his wife, "Sonia, this needs a father and son talk. Let me take care of this." Sonia nodded in agreement.

"Son, when you were little, we protected you from bad thresher sharks, big fish, and other sharks who bullied and teased you. Now, we will no longer do that, because we want you to learn how to defend and protect yourself."

"And for you to learn how to handle these bullies, you must face them yourself and let them know that you are better and smarter than they are," added Sonia.

"I know you told me that many times before that I have to ignore those bullies and that I should appear brave and strong like this!" Albee raised his snout, his front fins, and his tail.

"Good job, son—that's how you should appear—brave and strong," said Sonia.

Apo placing his snout near Albee's snout, "Son...think of yourself as better than them and remember as we already told you before, if they start to hurt you, swim away quickly. Do not fight unfriendly behavior with angry behavior, because it is not worth your time!"

Another white-bellied eagle flying above heard the talk between Apo and Albee and decided to interrupt, "Albee, swim away quickly...not worth your time akkk....akkk!" Then he grabbed an unsuspecting sardine with his claws and flew away.

"That white bird even agreed with me, son," said Apo while pointing his snout at the eagle.

"Okay, Dad and Mom, I will swim down myself. And where are you both going to be?"

"We will just be swimming around here and we will wait for you. We want to get report from you on how you handled those bullies," said Apo.

"Be careful, son, and remember to be smart, have courage, and stay strong," said Sonia as she touched Albee's head with her front fin.

"Okay, Mom...thanks."

As they were about to swim away, Sonia and Apo noticed Albee spinning around, unable to decide which direction to go to.

"Albee, please make up your mind now!" yelled Sonia.

"Okay, Mom and Dad, I am diving down then...bye."

Sonia was bothered by Albee's unsure action.

"Apo, Albee is such a compassionate shark, but he cannot make up his mind...I am worried."

"That action is telling us that it is now time for Albee to grow up, develop his inner strength, and meet other sea creatures. Maybe they will learn to like him. If he needs us for anything, we are always here for him."

"Well...let's try that." Then Sonia and Apo dove up and down chasing the elusive flying fish.

As Albee approached the tall sea grass, he forgot for a moment what he craved. Instead, he paused to watch the swaying sea grass that looked like dancers moving to the rhythm of the rushing waves.

"Oh...oh...oh, I forgot that I am here to get some shrimp!" He pushed himself between the sea grasses and saw a colony of shrimp near the bottom. He opened his mouth preparing to gulp a big heaping pile, but the shrimp disappeared without warning as another big brown mouth slurped the colony of shrimp ahead of him!

"Hah! I beat you, ugly shark...now it's my turn to finish you!" The huge brown catfish showed Albee his large sharp teeth.

"Mr. Catfish and Albee"

"Oh no! You cannot hurt me Mr. Catfish, because I am an albino shark and I am more special than you!" Albee protested, as he pretended to be brave.

"Who told you that?" asked Mr. Catfish while moving closer.

"My mom and dad and I will ask them to come down to tell you."

"You better hurry, because I have no time to wait," warned the catfish. Then he flipped his lower fins to signal Albee to leave quickly.

"Okay, I will," said a scared Albee and he swam away swiftly. He went to the spot where he thought his mom and dad were.

Instead, he saw Rico and Max, the two young bigger thresher sharks that were bullies. They blocked his path and confronted him.

"Albee, you do not look like us! You had better move far away where weird sharks like you live. We do not want you in Malapascua. You bring us bad luck!" said Rico.

"Yes, you need to go away because you are white and ghastly and your eyes are big and ugly!" echoed Max, the second thresher shark.

Several seahorses, angelfish, and small blue crabs saw what was going on and they quickly hid behind and under a large black stone.

"Rico and Max, you are not being nice! I am a thresher shark like you, but somewhat different because of my creamy skin! I have eyes like you but a little bigger. These are things I cannot change. I don't understand about this bad luck thing. Why should I go away when I was born in this sea!" Albee raised his snout and fins to show anger.

Without warning, Rico swung his tail towards Albee's side, but missed it. Max sneaked under Albee, then bumped his belly hard with his snout.

"Ouch, that hurts. You both are mean!"

Max and Rico swung their tails ready to smack Albee when a very large manta ray passed by.

"Hey...hey, stop! What are you both doing to this small shark? Just because you are bigger, you will bully and hurt those smaller than you? Who taught you this bad behavior?"

"Nobody," said Rico with his snout down.

"What about you, you other shark?"

"Nobody," said Max also with snout down.

"But Mr. Manta, we do not like him, because he looks different," protested Rico.

"Yes, he just looks weird and ugly, so he should go away," added Max.

"You both need to learn some lessons in good behavior."

Albee nodded in agreement and swam closer to the manta ray, shaking.

"Mr. Manta Ray, my name is Albee and thank you very much for your kind help."

"No problem, Albee, you go now and I will take care of this two and goodbye!"

Albee quickly swam to the surface and spotted his mom and dad who were 'fish hunting' for Pacific whiting.

"Mom and Dad, I was attacked by Rico and Max and challenged by an angry catfish! A manta ray helped me escaped from Rico and Max's meanness!"

"These bullies are truly irresponsible, they could hurt you. Did you use the trick that we talked about?" Apo asked.

"Well...somewhat, but why do I look different, Mom and Dad? Now...I do not even have a friend... friends would be better."

"Son, you are the same as other thresher sharks, even if your color is different." Sonia then stroked Albee's head with her right fin. "We just want to let you know that you are a special shark. Your dad and I love you and are very proud of you. We don't care what those bullies said about you."

"How about friends? Nobody likes me, because I looked different!"

Apo spoke out, "Son, just be patient, because you will eventually find a friend someday...someone you will like."

"When is this going to happen?" demanded Albee.

Sonia calmly said, "Well, we do not know when, but those who patiently wait will eventually have friends. A true friend is hard to find and it's better to wait than rush to find one. We understand you are bullied and teased and it makes us sad too."

"Albee, do understand that those bullies and teasers lacked discipline. They bully and tease others, because they are not sure about themselves and they want attention. They think this is the only way to do it," said Apo.

In an approving tone Albee said, "I understand, Mom and Dad...I love you both too. Maybe I should separate from you more often, so that I can build my inner strength and then maybe I can find good friends."

"Perfect idea, Albee, and we're glad that you thought of it first. Please be careful and always remember what I told you about protecting yourself. Do not challenge big fish, because they might hurt you," warned Apo. "Now your mom and I will go to the Monad Shoal to relax and see our friends, the wrasse fish."

"Bye, Mom and Dad, and have fun."

Then Apo and Sonia swam toward Monad Shoal, a plateau not far from Malapascua.

Thresher sharks love to visit this underwater plateau. It is located not far from Malapascua and it is here that wrasse fish 'sort of cleaned them' by removing parasites from their skin and 'junks' from their gills and mouth and then used them for food! Think of Monad Shoal as a car washing station and dental office for the sharks...and a 'buffet restaurant' for the wrasse fish! Because of their give-and-take relationship, the thresher sharks would not even think of eating these small wrasse fish.

Down in the deep, Albee was swimming away slowly when suddenly a young silvertip shark attacked him from the right side.

"You are a show-off...jumping very high in front of humans!"

"But I was made to jump and it just happened that I can jump higher than other threshers!" explained Albee.

"I don't care...but you better go somewhere else!" Then the silvertip attacked him again from behind. Albee turned around to check his tail just to make sure it was still there. He leaped very high and landed with a big splash...then disappeared in a flash. The silvertip swam away unhappy, but promised to get rid of Albee someday.

CHAPTER FOUR

Albee Entertained and Helped Ian

Albee did not know that his high leap Io escape from the silvertip entertained the tourists, visitors, and children. Those who were at Lagoon Park clapped with excitement and yelled, "Oh, Albee, that was awesome!" Some children in the park chimed, "That was quite amazing!"

The passengers on the glass-bottom boats and catamarans witnessed what Albee just did and yelled, "Wow…. wowie…awesome! Albee, very stunning!"

A four-year-old blond-haired autistic boy named Ian was vacationing in Malapascua from Australia with his mom Jean, dad Brad, and older sister Emily. They were in a catamaran for an Albee sighting excursion trip when Albee suddenly jumped fifty feet from their boat! There was excitement from everyone and the "Ohhs, ahhhs, wow, what a delight, and awesome" were repeated many times over.

Ian who was sitting next to Emily looked at the children who were in the boat then blurted, "Oh wow!! Is awesome delight, Albee!" When Jean, Brad, and Emily heard what Ian just said, they were very surprised to hear him speak the words clearly, instead of garbled.

"Ian, Emily, Mom Jean and Dad Brad in Malapascua"

"Mom did you hear that? Ian talked...it's even clear talk!" Emily beamed with excitement and clapped her hands.

With tears streaming down Jean's eyes, she stood up, scooped Ian, then hugged and kissed him. Brad stood up too, but was speechless. While gently stroking Ian's back, Jean said, "Son, you finally talked. Brad, honey, Ian is finally talking!"

"Jean and Emily, we should be thankful for Albee. Let's visit Malapascua more often. Maybe Ian could pick up some more words," suggested Brad.

Suddenly the captain yelled, "Okay, you all sit down...we are going back to shore now!"

CHAPTER FIVE

Albee Day Celebration

Albee swimming not far away from the beach heard music, laughter, and singing.
"Oh, some human noise...I'd better swim closer to shore." He was surprised to see a big poster of himself on the stage with his name printed underneath. There were small photos of thresher sharks around him, but his photo was the biggest! Big signs were all over Lagoon Beach Park, which read, "ALBEE FIESTA DAY." He also saw balloons that looked like him and children happily playing with them. He even saw several people wearing T-shirts with pictures of himself. He saw children with their moms and dads swimming at the park's lagoon using Albee floats. There was a man-made slide secured on a large rock. Albee saw a full image of himself perched on the top.

"Hmmm, I must be special to humans," he thought.

Then he saw a man behind a refreshment booth yelling, "Albee refreshing drinks and popsicles! Come and enjoy them, made from finest Pascua citrus and local fruit juice!" Children with their parents were lining up to buy Albee drinks and ice pops. While waiting for their treat, kids were giggling and jumping, pretending to be Albee.

"Oh this tastes very good and refreshing!" said one female tourist from Korea.

"Momma, I'm hot...I want Albee pop," pleaded a five-year-old girl to her mom as she wiped sweats from her forehead from a pink Albee shirt she was wearing. Her mom handed her the pop. As she started licking, the sweat on her forehead magically disappeared!!

"This tastes good and yummy, Mommy."

Albee thought, "Oh...I must be really special after all! Mom and Dad were right." Then he paused, "And that's how Mom and Dad got to name me 'ALBEE'...maybe from that picture?"

Suddenly, a glass-bottom boat was heading towards Albee carrying a boatload of tourists. He quickly swam underwater and rested near a rock. Then the white sand not far from him stirred and out came Lukas, who appeared angry and hissed at him.

"You must be Lukas, the white crocodile," said Albee, who was quite surprised. He tried not to look scared.

"You must be Albee and I do not like that you steal the attention away from me. Humans are no longer coming to see me and I am mad and jealous. I want to challenge you to a fight," said an angry Lukas.

"I did not tell these humans to come and see me, Lukas. But why do you want to fight, when we can just talk in peace?"

"BECAUSE I WANT TO PROVE TO YOU AND TO THEM THAT I AM BIGGER AND STRONGER AND I AM THE KING OF ALL!! THEREFORE, THE ATTENTION SHOULD BE ON ME, NOT ON YOU!!"

"Sorry, Lukas, I do not feel like fighting a 'KING' today, but maybe next time… bye."

"Well, I will just eat you then!" announced Lukas as he showed his dirty sharp teeth.

Albee thought quickly, "Lukas, I don't think this is the best time to eat me, because it's breakfast. I will taste better if you eat me either at lunch or dinner… just look at the sun above."

While Lukas checked where the sun was, Albee swam away very quickly. Lukas chased him, but could not catch up with Albee who swam faster. To scare Lukas, Albee jumped very high and made a big splash, just missing a tourist boat.

Lukas was not happy that Albee had gotten away. He roared, then yelled, "I am not done with you, Albee! I will wait for you night and day!" Then he swam away very mad and very angry.

CHAPTER SIX

Albee Met Bennie

Meanwhile, the tourists in the boat were wet from Albee's splash. "That white shark almost hit us and I'm wet, including my camera. His jump was awesome though," said a Chinese tourist, while wiping the camera with his handkerchief.

"Oh wow, very nice jump, Albee!" said a young male visitor from Manila.

Albee's leap may have amused the tourists, but not the two fishermen nearby, who were startled by Albee's jump. They lost their grip on the homemade crab trap full of blue crabs and down it fell, back into the sea. The strong crash opened the latch and the crabs swam free.

The fishermen were upset at their misfortune and blamed each other for being clumsy. They argued and pointed at each other and even said rude words. Albee regretted his mistake, but he was not capable of saying "Sorry" to humans. Tired of blaming, the fishermen stopped arguing, turned on their engine, and sped away zigzagging.

Albee with Bennie the crab

One of the crabs that escaped was moaning and groaning…"Oh my back hurts…those crabs were stepping on my back!"

Albee swam closer to find out. "What happened to you?"

"Well…I tried to join those crabs because I wanted to be their friend. While we were following Jose, the leader crab, he entered a trap that had a chicken neck and pig's feet hanging on wires! Once we were inside the trap, they were mad at me for giving them bad luck! Then told me that they did not like me, because I am too blue to be a real blue crab!" said the crab pointing his large pinchers to his upper shell.

"Well, let me bring you to a safer place before a big fish eats you." He let the blue crab hop on his back.

"It sounds like you will not eat me, but when you take me down, make sure there's plenty of seaweed…that would make it softer for my body," demanded the blue crab.

While making their descent Albee said, "Well, I will try to find one, but can you just be satisfied with what is available?"

"Well, it depends on my mood. By the way, my name is Benito or Bennie for short…what is yours?"

"I am Albee and I am an albino thresher shark." Just then, Albee found a perfect spot for Bennie. "Are you hungry, Bennie?"

"I am hungry, but do not give me a dead or almost dead fish, because it does not taste good and I don't like it!"

"Bennie...you cannot be picky. Please just be happy that I will find food for you."

"Okay, almost dead is fine," responded Bennie in a snappy way.

Albee left quickly, brought back six almost dead sardines, holding them between his teeth. They were both so hungry that it took them only few minutes to munch on the fish.

"Albee, I feel like I owe you big for saving my life. Why don't I become your new friend?"

"But my friend should be another thresher shark—not a crab!" Albee protested.

"But don't you already have a shark friend?" asked a curious Bennie.

"No...nobody likes me, because I looked different...see!" Albee turned from side to side to show Bennie.

"Well...nobody likes me either, because I am too blue to be a real blue crab!" Bennie spun around to show Albee how blue he was.

"Well, I guess you are right, Bennie. Maybe we ought to be friends."

Then Albee paused for a moment, "I remember what my mom and dad said, that someday...I would eventually find a friend, someone I will like."

An excited Bennie asked, "Your mom and dad were referring to me?"

"Not exactly but... ...at least I now have a crab friend."

The next day, Bennie suggested to Albee that they go to a cave where squid liked to hang out. These large squid do not like trespassers, so any uninvited sea creatures that enter the cave will get a barrage of black ink squirts.

"Albee...this is perfect, because once those squids see you, especially if you scare them, they will squirt ink at you and voila! Your skin color will be changed and you'll look like a normal thresher shark!"

Albee liked the idea, but insisted that he ask his parent's permission first.

"Albee, you should be able to decide for yourself!" insisted Bennie.

"I do not know...I just can't make up my mind," said a confused Albee.

"Where are they? Let me convince them myself, because nobody will ever say no to me!" said Bennie bragging.

"No, I want to tell them first and if they say "no" then convince them for me, okay?"

"Fine, if that's what you want, Albee."

They both went to the Monad Shoal where Albee's parents were relaxing while the wrasse fish cleaned them.

"What? Whose idea is this?" demanded Apo.

"From my new friend, Bennie the crab."

"Oh, you finally found a friend, Albee?" Sonia asked.

"Yes, Mom, his name is Bennie the crab." Albee turned, then called Bennie, who did not hear Albee's first call, because he was busy devouring the tail of a still wiggling shrimp.

He called again, "Bennie, come out from that coral and meet my mom and dad."

Bennie completed his meal and swam briskly toward Albee to meet his parents.

"Apo and Sonia, if you truly love Albee, you should really let him try my idea. If it works, then he will become a normal thresher shark. But if not...at least we tried."

"Bennie, you do have a quick wit and are somewhat convincing. If it makes Albee happy, I guess there's no harm in trying. But we will go with you to witness the change in Albee's look," said Sonia.

CHAPTER SEVEN

The Cave, Earthquake, and Lukas

At the southernmost tip of Malapascua was a cave formed from a volcanic eruption thousands of years ago. The cave and the surrounding area were popular with different fish species, sharks, scuba divers, and tourists. Although both large and small squid were the main residents of the cave, other marine life such as sea horses, red and blue crabs, shrimp, pompano fish, and other small sea creatures lived there too.

"Okay, Sonia and Apo, I will lead the way, then the three of you follow," said Bennie. As Bennie, Apo, and Sonia were entering the cave, Albee, who was about to enter, was distracted by yelling tourists and a bright light from a glass-bottom boat used by operators for tourists to enjoy the view of underwater life. Albee turned around and swam toward the light.

"Let me check first what is going on. Oh, I love that bright light!"

"Albee...come and follow us now, son!" yelled Apo.

Albee swam back, "Okay, Dad, I am coming!" As Albee was about to enter the cave, a strong earthquake shook Malapascua Island. Large volcanic rocks toppled and closed off the entrance to the cave.

The glass-bottom boat swayed back and forth.

"Help! Help! We're all going to die," screamed a male tourist. Children cried, scared and confused. Other tourists were scared too!

"Sir, please relax. You are making everyone nervous," pleaded the captain. Then the boat stopped swaying. "Everyone please calm down...we are going back now, so please hold on to your kids," advised the captain. Boats after boats were speeding to shore with terrified tourists on board.

Meanwhile at the cave, Albee was taken aback and shaken from the force of large rocks falling in front of him.

"What...what happened?" he asked a group of pompano fish and a manta ray who were nearby, also shaken.

One pompano said, "I am not sure, but we were about to enter that cave and it's a good thing we did not, because we would have been gone by now!"

"That's right! My mom and dad and my friend, Bennie, are inside!" Oh my...what shall I do now?" said a worried Albee.

A papa dolphin swimming with his family interjected, "If they are inside that cave, better prepare for the worst, kid."

Albee paused for a moment and shed some shark tears.

"This is all my fault...it's all my fault! Instead of accepting who I am...I was too stubborn! Now my mom and dad and my friend, Bennie, are gone forever!" Suddenly, Albee heard a familiar voice.

"No, I am not gone forever yet."

He turned around and saw Bennie swimming toward him. "Bennie...you are okay!"

"Yes, I'm still here and that's the best thing of being smaller. I pushed myself against a small opening and a large squid gave me a boost."

"What about my mom and dad! Where are they?"

"Well...I tried to help them get out, but the opening was too small for them."

"Poor mom and dad. I wish I could move those large rocks! Did they say anything to you before you left them?"

"They told me that if they cannot come out of the cave alive, I was to tell you that they love you and to continue to be a brave, smart, and strong shark."

Albee turned around and swam slowly away from the cave while Bennie followed from behind.

"Albee, are you going to blame me?"

"No, Bennie, I am not blaming you...I actually blame myself for not accepting who I am. Therefore, from now on I will not do a thing to change me."

"Thank you, Albee, for not blaming me."

"You're welcome, Bennie, but I will surely miss my mom and dad, who tried their best to be good parents."

"Well, it's just you and me now and I think we should continue to be friends," Bennie suggested.

"I do not mind that we hang out together, but with my mom and dad gone and me being bullied and teased, I would like to move to Torabeles Sea where Uncle Baldo, my dad's brother, lived. When he came to visit us, and my dad and I visited him, he made me feel like I was his own son. Would you like to come with me, Bennie?"

"Torabeles Sea! Albee, where is this place? It sounds like the territory of scary sea monsters!"

"Well, Bennie, I cannot tell you where, but we followed the ship's route, which brought us directly to Torabeles. There are no monsters but plenty of ships...big and small."

"Albee, are we going to meet some dangers on the way and maybe that would be the end of us?"

"Well, no more dangerous than what we have encountered here in Malapascua. We just have to be strong, smart, and careful—just like my mom and dad always reminded me."

"Oh no...Oh no! You go yourself, Albee, because I am not leaving Malapascua."

Suddenly, Lukas came out of the sand showing his sharp dirty teeth to Albee and Bennie, who were taken aback.

"So, Albee, you are leaving Malapascua—that's good, because I will now be the center of attention!" declared an angry Lukas.

"But, Lukas, the tourists are afraid of you and they do not even like you. Why don't you go back to where you came from?" suggested Albee.

"That's right, Lukas, you are a troublemaker," added Bennie.

"I am not a troublemaker! I am mad, because humans threw sticks at me and told me to go away. They would rather see Albee than me!" said an angry Lukas. Then he added, "I am showing my teeth to let you know that I am ready to eat both of you right now." Lukas started swimming toward Albee and Bennie.

"Bennie, hop on my back, quick," urged Albee. A chase ensued. Lukas aimed for Albee's tail, but it moved so hard and fast that Lukas wished it would not last.

"Bennie, hang on tight, because I will make a high jump."

"Okay, Albee. A high jump and a big splash!"

16

"Oh my eyes...my eyes they're burning from that nasty salty water!" Lukas whined while rubbing his eyes with his front legs. He grunted and roared, "I still have time to catch up with you two!" warned Lukas to no one, because Albee and Bennie were long gone.

CHAPTER 8

Albee Entertained Again

"Mommy! Daddy! Emily! Did you see Albee with a crab on his back? That was awesome!" yelled Ian.

"Oh yeah, Ian...very awesome!" said an excited Emily.

"Yes, sweetheart, but why a crab on Albee's back, Brad?" asked Jean.

"I don't know, Jean, but it was an awesome sight indeed."

Then they heard Ian kept repeating, "Awesome, awesome, Albee. I love you, Albee, I wish you would jump again." Jean, Brad, and Emily beamed with happiness when they heard Ian's wish.

Meanwhile, looking tired and exhausted from the chase, Albee and Bennie rested on a big rock near a coral reef.

"You see, Bennie, Lukas is really a dangerous crocodile and I surely will not miss him. Why don't you change your mind and come with me to Torabeles?"

"Albee, I was born in Malapascua and I am not leaving my birthplace. Lukas may look mean, but he is actually not a smart croc."

"What makes you say that, Bennie?"

"Some fish told me that if you tell Lucas his teeth are not white enough or that he has many cavities, he will let you go, instead of eating you. Then he will rub his teeth hard on the roughest coral—sort of brushing his teeth like humans."

"Lukas is indeed a gullible crocodile. I played a trick on him that also worked when I told him I was not good to eat for breakfast. But, Bennie, why did you not tell me *before* he chased us?"

"Albee, I do not want to take any chances. What if those fish had lied and we were already in Lukas' mouth? Then, what would we do?"

"Yeah, you're right, Bennie. We would surely be his lunch or dinner, whatever time of the day it was. Well, enough of Lukas, but since you are not coming with me, Bennie, I will go to Torabeles alone." Stroking Bennie with his front fin, Albee said, "I am just happy I found a friend, even if our friendship is short-lived, but I will always remember you. Bye, Bennie."

"Please be careful, Albee. I will remember you too, my friend."

Then Albee turned around and followed the maritime route without spinning around this time, so he swam directly to where he was supposed to go. Bennie released large bubbles from his mouth—it's a crab way of expressing being upset and sad.

CHAPTER 9

Good-Bye, Malapascua

Albee with Bennie on his back entered Zulu sea and the water started to get choppy.
"See…if you did not ride on my back, you would have been carried away by those waves," said Albee.

"Well I was forced to do this, because you told me I was a slow swimmer. Next time, do not call me a 'slow swimmer,' okay?"

"Whatever you say, slow swimmer!" Albee chuckled.

Bennie tried to change the subject.

"Albee, have you ever wondered why I decided to come with you instead?"

"No, Bennie, please tell me."

"Well, have you heard of the saying…'friends in need are friends indeed'?"

"No, Bennie, please explain."

"Well, Albee, I just couldn't let you go alone, because you might need me and I still have this guilty feeling of bringing your parents into that cave."

"Bennie, I understand you were just doing what was best for me. There's always a reason for everything, please do not blame yourself."

"Thanks, Albee."

"You see, Bennie, I was too dependent on Mom and Dad—I cannot even decide things for myself. It is now time for me to be brave, strong, and smart. I'm going to live with my parent's wish…it's good for me."

Suddenly, from a distance Bennie spotted a very familiar sight. "Albee, there are very low-hanging fishing nets ahead. These nets are dangerous for us and we had better be careful."

"What should we do, Bennie? This is the best route to the Torabeles Sea!"

"Well, here's my plan. I will get off your back and we both swim very slowly below those nets, but try not to wiggle your tail, okay?"

"Okay, Bennie, just tell me where to go."

Several blue crabs also crawled below the fishing nets, so they would not be caught in them.

As Albee and Bennie were about to pass the last net, Albee forgot not to wiggle his tail and got tangled. There were several fish species already trapped in the net yelling for help!!

"Bennie…my tail is tangled—please, help me!"

"Albee's tail in trouble"

Bennie turned around and saw Albee struggling to free himself. "Albee, just relax and do not tire yourself...I'll find a way."

Just then, the last of about 60 large crabs passed the last net.

"Hey, my fellow crabs, please help me free my friend!" yelled Bennie.

They turned around and saw a familiar shark.

"Hey, isn't that the white shark who freed us from the crab trap?" said Jose, the leader crab.

"Yes, that's Albee and I am Bennie who was with you in that crab trap. Jose, I need your help, quick."

Suddenly the net started to be hoisted up.

Albee and the fish in the net yelled for help.

"Help...help...we do not want to become sushi," screamed both Albee and a young bonito fish.

Then they yelled in fish chorus, "We do not want to be grilled fish either!"

Jose sensed the urgency of immediate action.

"Okay, gang, let's clip those nets with your biggest pinchers and do it quick, before we lose our friends. Clip on the count of a one, a two, a three, a four..."

Bennie started clipping but did not like Jose's slow count.

"Jose, your counting is too slow and you are not even helping! Those fish and Albee are in need of emergency help!! I want quick action now!" demanded Bennie.

"I am trying, Bennie, but I can't count fast and since I do the counting, I don't have to help with the clipping."

"Argh! Never mind," said an exasperated Bennie. Then he noticed the crabs were dawdling. Bennie became super mad and yelled, "Hey, crabs...why are you doing nothing?"

"Because Jose did not say anything!" answered the crabs.

Then Albee and the fishes yelled, "Hey, crabs! Please do something and stop arguing! This net keeps hoisting!"

"Okay, Jose, count faster, but do not count back to number one...go right at number eight and do it right now!" Bennie raised and then lowered his pinchers to signal Jose to start counting immediately.

"Okay, Bennie." Then he yelled, "Crabs, clip at the count of 8, 9, 10, 11, 12, 13, 14, 15, 16..." and the net ripped when it was about a foot above water. There was a big crash!! And a big splash!! Then down and farther down went Albee and the fish. They swam swiftly to the bottom of the sea making sure there will be no repeat of their scary misery. Bennie, Albee, and the fish expressed their appreciation to Jose and the crabs for their help. After saying 'good-bye,' they all continued on with their journey.

While above water, "Bozo, where are the fish and the shark?" asked the captain to his deckhand.

"Boss, first we got something...the net ripped, then we got nothing—we'd better stop fishing, because there will be nothing!" answered the deckhand in a sad tone.

"Bozo, you are nothing but a sad clown...always have excuse. Get another net and do not rip it this time. We need to catch more fish and sharks to deliver to our hungry customers," demanded the pot-bellied captain.

"Okay, Boss, another net coming right up!"

CHAPTER TEN

Seaweed Noodles and Malapascua with No Albee

"Albee, I'm tired, bored...and hungry. Are we almost there yet?"

"Well, maybe, but let's rest and grab some fish to eat," suggested Albee.

They circled around a very large coral reef with school upon school of fish, both big and small. Shrimp in various sizes and colors lined like rainbow against the backdrop of the clear blue water. They saw eels under the rocks and colorful sea anemones and other sea creatures resting on top.

"Albee, this buffet of yummy snacks makes me hungry."

"That's right, Bennie, we just happened to be lucky."

Suddenly a gang of mean-looking seaweed noodles wound around Albee's snout and fins, and on Bennie's pinchers and claws, but not in his mouth. The seaweed noodles tried to attach to Albee's tail, but he flipped it fast...very fast from side to side.

"His tail is moving very fast," said a cluster of noodles. "Forget it, let's go to his mouth," said another bunch of larger noodles.

"Albee, please help me...they're covering my eyes and I cannot see!" yelled Bennie, who tried to pull the noodles with his pinchers, but the noodles' grip was quite strong.

Sea Noodles Attacked Albee and Bennie

Albee briskly moved his snout up and down...side to side and soon freed up his mouth from the strong grip of the noodles. In his anger, he chewed the seaweed noodles that entered his mouth and noticed that they tasted good. He munched...and munched until the noodles loosened their grip. They all drifted away scared...then slowly disappeared.

"Bennie, catch the end of the noodle with your free claws and start eating it...it tastes good anyway."

Bennie did as Albee instructed and the seaweed noodles also loosened their grip on Bennie's claws and began to drift away.

"Whew! That was close, Albee. I'm glad that you thought of eating those seaweed noodles instead of fighting them."

"Well, I remember my dad said I should not fight attackers with counterattack. But whether that would apply to the seaweed noodles, I don't know."

Far away in Malapascua, the local residents, tourists, visitors, and children, including Ian's family, were wondering why there were no more sightings of Albee.

With Albee gone, Lukas found an opportunity. "Ha...ha...ha, I will now be the center of attention in Malapascua and I will be the king of all sea creatures!" He emerged right in front of a tourist boat with his head and teeth sticking out supposedly to smile and pose. Some fish species nearby saw Lukas and they all swam away scared.

The frantic tourists and visitors yelled, "Help...help, this croc with ugly dirty teeth is going to eat us!"

"Oh, that is just Lukas, the angry white crocodile, and he is mean. He is not supposed to be in Malapascua. He is from the island of Pilar!" said a mama visitor from a nearby town.

Brad and Jean hugged Ian and Emily.

"Mommy, I'm scared of that ugly croc," complained Emily.

"Me too, I don't like that ugly crocodile...I like Albee. Mom, where is Albee?" Ian asked.

"I don't know, son, but we will try to find out when we arrive at the shore."

"Yes, children, we will try to find out," added Brad.

"Captain, let's go back to shore now. We're afraid of that ugly white croc," suggested a papa tourist.

Lukas did not like being called ugly.

"Okay, you called me ugly...we'll see!" He slammed his tail on the side of the boat and tipped it a bit to the right. Everyone screamed and called for help.

"Okay, hang on tight, we're going back," assured the captain. But before he turned on the engine, he tossed a large stick onto Lukas' head and then with a 'thump' and a 'bump' Lukas swam underwater angrier than ever, but not bitter.

"Someday, humans will see me as better looking than Albee. I will charm them with my nice smile and maybe a side view pose this time," said Lukas while facing in front of a sunken vessel's glass window.

The tourist and visitors were concerned that Lukas the croc would show up again. Scared and shaken, they demanded that the captain leave for shore immediately. He started the engine and the catamaran roared like thunder, startling those divers that were underwater.

"I do not think I will come back to Malapascua, if it's only that ugly croc and no Albee," said a lady visitor. Every tourist and visitor in the boat, including Ian, Emily, Brad, and Jean were not happy at Albee's absence and totally agreed with what the lady visitor was saying.

CHAPTER ELEVEN

No More Tourists and Visitors

The mayor and town officials of Malapascua instructed divers and fishermen to find Albee.

"Mr. Mayor, sir, and madam officials...sorry, we cannot find Albee. We turned rocks, entered caves, and searched everywhere, but we cannot find Albee," said the divers and fishermen.

"We found an angry Lukas. He chased us fast, but we got away by hitting his head with a rock," said the leader of the diving team.

"I do not know what to do anymore...Albee helped our economy and there were plenty of jobs and now he is gone! We have nothing!" Mr. Tambokon, the pot-bellied mayor, sobbed and then sank his head on the table. After a few minutes, he raised his head and said to the council members, "Nobody likes to swim in our beautiful beaches anymore, because they are scared of Lukas. The tourists and visitors are gone, we have to find Albee and get rid of Lukas, the mean croc. He is not from Malapascua!"

"Mr. Tambokon, maybe we should donate Lukas to the Manila Zoo," suggested one of the female council members.

Another male council member added, "Maybe Albee was afraid of Lukas and he might come back if Lukas is gone."

"Brilliant idea, brilliant idea...let's do it," said a perked-up mayor.

Meanwhile, restaurants and hotels were almost empty and many islanders lost their jobs. Without steady jobs, the inhabitants went back to fishing. To catch more fish to sell, fishermen used dynamite to kill all kinds of fish and sharks—small, big, baby, pregnant, and even the poisonous puffer fish. The dynamite blast also damaged some coral reefs in Malapascua. There were fishermen who lost their arms, legs, became blind, and even were killed from the premature blast of the dynamite. But this did not stop other fishermen from doing it again and again!

Angry local inhabitants lined up in front of the city hall and demanded, "Mr. Mayor and council members, you need to do something about this dynamite fishing and you'd better do it quick! Also, we need jobs...our kids are hungry and so are we!"

"But our tourists and visitors are gone, so I cannot afford to pay the coast guard. We only have few policemen and we cannot police everyone. The tourists and visitors helped our economy, but with Albee gone, they are not coming back. I do not know what to do anymore!" Mr. Tambokon lamented. The five council members nodded in agreement, but did not say anything.

Meanwhile, the fish species, sharks, and even Lukas were afraid to swim on the surface because of the loud dynamite blasts.

"Lukas, I thought you were tough, so why are you hiding under the sand?" asked a grouper fish.

"I cannot stand loud noises, it hurts my ears. Maybe I should go back to Pilar." Lucas complained.

"Maybe you should, Lukas," said the grouper fish.

One day the marine species had a gathering to discuss what to do with this almost daily dynamite blast.

Rico who wanted Albee to go away said, "I was glad that Albee no longer lived in Malapascua, but it seems that this dynamite blast started when he left. I do not know why."

"That's right…we will all die from these loud blasts. I saw several dead fish already and we will be next!" said Max, the thresher shark that once bullied and teased Albee.

"Maybe we should ask every sea creature to spread the message around until it reaches Albee, that we want him to come back," suggested the silvertip shark that once accused Albee of being a show-off. Everyone agreed with the suggestion.

Then the sea creatures started the task of spreading the message from shark to shark, shark to fish, fish to fish, fish to squid, squid to squid…. and so on.

CHAPTER TWELVE

Toblee Green Plant Extract

Far away, Bennie and Albee were nearing Torabeles Sea. A short distance from them, they noticed two fishermen pouring a bucketful of 'green stuff' into the water. They kept swimming, not knowing that danger was ahead of them.

Suddenly, Albee slowed down. "Bennie I can hardly breathe, please help me."

"Albee, what is happening?"

"I do not know, but I am weak and it's hard to breath," whispered an almost limp Albee.

Just then, Bennie spotted five cormorants fishing underwater and asked them to help move Albee out of the green stuff. The cormorants agreed, but pulling Albee with their small beaks was quite difficult for the birds. Luckily, a large wake from a coast guard's boat helped push Albee out of the danger zone. Bennie thanked the cormorants and away they flew with fish in each of their mouths. Albee felt better after a few minutes.

"I am suspicious of that 'green stuff' and luckily I was not affected," said Bennie.

"There must be a reason for this, Bennie. Maybe something is being planned for us," answered a weak Albee.

While above water, the coast guard approached the two fishermen and arrested them for illegal fishing by using the extract of a plant called 'toblee.' The fishermen went to jail and were fined $50,000.00 each!

The extract cuts off the oxygen supply, so that fish will stop breathing and die. The fish are still safe to eat, but the illegal fishing practice will kill other fish and sharks: big, small, pregnant and not pregnant, and even poisonous fish, but not crustaceans, like Bennie.

"Bennie, thanks for saving my life. I'm glad you came with me. Had it not been for your quick action, I would probably have died. Thanks for your help, my good friend." Albee slowly flipped his weak fins.

"Well…that's what friends are for," said Bennie with a crab smile.

CHAPTER THIRTEEN

Torabeles Sea Pollution

After three days of swimming, Albee and Bennie finally arrived at their destination. There were large and small ships, and even speedboats crisscrossing the channels of Torabeles Sea. Both boats and ships were dumping garbage and sewage into the ocean, making the water dirty and murky.

"Albee, is this where you want to live? Look at those floating bottles, papers everywhere, old tires—oh my! Too much junk to mention!" exclaimed Bennie without realizing that some shoelaces were hanging on his pinchers.

"Bennie, let me pull those shoelaces off, before they hurt you." After Albee pulled the shoelaces with his teeth, he noticed that Bennie was very angry.

"See! These humans are not even thinking about the dangers that we are facing! We could die from their irresponsible behavior!" said an enraged Bennie.

"I totally agree with you, Bennie, and I wished humans would change bad practices that can harm us."

"Albee, I really do not know what these humans are thinking. Look what they did to this water! It's so muddy and yucky!" Bennie kept trying to shake off some globs of brown 'stuff' that were sticking onto his claws.

"When I used to come here with my dad, this water was very clear and nice like Malapascua. I do not know what happened."

"Well, I know what happened," said an angry Bennie.

"What do you know, Bennie?"

"Did you see the garbage and sewage thrown from those ships and boats? That is the very reason why this water is no longer clear!"

"That...and humans who do not care is another big reason, Bennie."

Then they finally arrived at the place where Albee's Uncle Baldo lived. Albee and Bennie went from artificial reefs to sunken ships, to a cement pillar from a building and a pile of wood to underwater small caves, but only a few fish species were left. They asked the catfish and carps, now the dominant species in the area, about his Uncle Baldo, but nobody knew him. They went further south where the water was still a bit clear and finally a mature thresher shark told Albee the sad truth.

"Albee, your Uncle Baldo was hit by a propeller from a fast running speedboat. He was my best friend and I'm still upset at what happened to him."

He thanked the mature thresher, but the sad news hit Albee hard. Luckily, Bennie was there to console him.

"Bennie, let's go back to Malapascua where the water is clear and blue and no speeding boats and ships can hurt us."

"Good idea, Albee."

CHAPTER FOURTEEN

Albee and Bennie Returned with Minda

They were already past the busy channel of Torabeles Sea when they spotted a young albino thresher shark. The body was creamy, but the fins had some light-violet shading. The young shark was trying to shake the seaweed noodles from its mouth. Albee and Bennie rushed to help and started eating the seaweed noodles. The noodles loosened their grip and quickly drifted, then disappeared within minutes.

"Thanks for saving my life...my name is Minda. What's yours?"

"My name is Albee and I am also an albino like you. This is my friend, Bennie the crab."

"Glad to meet both of you. Where are you going?"

"Well...we are from Malapascua and we are going back, because we love the water there. It's very clear and blue and... no garbage!" said Bennie while pointing his claws toward Torabeles.

Albee, Minda and Bennie

"That's true, Minda. Malapascua is the perfect place for us," added Albee.

"Oh, I would love to move to Malapascua. Torabeles Sea is too polluted and junk's everywhere. Some of my dolphin friends died from plastic bags, soda cans, and other garbage thrown by humans. A couple of my fish friends and turtles died from fishing lines, nets, hooks, and from plastic drink holders discarded by reckless fishermen!"

"I bet some also died from careless boat operators like this one coming towards us." Albee was pointing his snout at a speedboat quickly closing in on them. Suddenly the boat's wake pushed the three of them near another speedboat.

"How could humans do this to us?" said Bennie, upset and angry, while trying to shake some shredded papers clinging to his claws.

"That speedboat almost hit mama, papa, and baby dolphins! This place has danger written all over it. Any more sea creatures hit by these speedboats, Minda?" asked Albee.

"Sure, I just saw two dolphins yesterday injured after being hit from a very fast running boat. Two bad sharks circled around them and both were gone in minutes. I'm afraid I will be next, so that is why I am moving away from this dangerous sea!"

"Well, that is really sad. Humans are trying to destroy our environment and pretty soon they will have no sea creatures to enjoy," said Bennie.

"That is right, we die because of careless human behavior and it should not be that way," echoed Albee.

"If they care about themselves, they should care about us too," Minda said while pointing her snout at another speedboat.

"You made a very good point, Minda. By the way, you are welcome to come and join with us. But don't you want to ask your mom and dad first if it's okay to move?" asked Albee.

"No, I don't have to ask my parents, because I know what is best for me and I can decide for myself," said a confident Minda.

"Okay, let's go—it's time to swim. Bennie and Minda, follow me!"

Meanwhile, it was sunny morning in Malapascua, where owners of almost empty hotels and restaurants were counting their meager earnings from yesterday. One hotel owner's dog, sensing the sadness of his master, moaned and groaned as he lay near his feet.

Ian's family was one of the few hotel guests that day. After breakfast, Jean and Brad took Ian and Emily to the dock, hoping to have a glimpse of Albee. After one hour of waiting, his mom and dad decided to go back to the hotel to get some drinks, but left Emily and Ian at the dock with their life vests on. Ian was sitting on a small picnic table playing with his small toy cars, including some Albee toys. He lined them up, as if these toys were about to enter a battle. Emily was playing with her doll, when she looked up and saw two albino thresher sharks jumping not far from her. Ian saw it too!

An excited Ian yelled, "I see Albee and another Albee—wow!" Other hotel guests that were on the dock saw the leap and recognized Albee right away, but were wondering why there was a second one.

Emily ran to the hotel, huffing and puffing to yell, "Mom and Dad...Albee is back and there's also another Albee, but it looks a little different!" They all ran to the dock to check it out.

The news spread quickly throughout Malapascua about the return of Albee and another thresher shark that was also an albino. News coverage of Albee and Minda on television and radio brought tourists and visitors back to Malapascua Island. Hotels and restaurants were almost always full.

The return of Albee with Minda brought economic prosperity to Malapascua once again. The mayor, council members, and inhabitants of Malapascua were very happy that there were now more jobs for everyone in the island. They held a street party in honor of Albee and Minda. There was singing, dancing, and laughter everywhere.

"This is the happiest day of my life," said a smiling mayor.

He ordered the fishermen using dynamites to be put to jail. Some were blind, some no longer had arms and legs, and some had even lost their ears! They pleaded for mercy, but Mr. Tambokon told them that many fish were killed because of their merciless activity and they were not even sorry. They groped and limped on the way to their jail cells with some assistance from the newly hired policemen on duty.

One day while Lukas was trying to catch some flying fish for food, he heard 'fish talk' that he did not like to hear.

"So Albee is back! Now is the time for me to finish him." Then, he saw two large dead chickens hanging not far from where he was.

"Oh! What are those?" He swam closer. "Chickens! My favorite! I am hungry and those flying fish are hard to catch anyway." Lukas grabbed the first chicken with his sharp teeth when he suddenly heard a loud boom and a sudden click.

"Someone is playing tricks on me and I blame humans and Albee!" The strong big net hoisted him up…and up. "What is going on?" He thrashed his whole body up and down, left and right, wanting to be set free from the hoisting net. He hissed and roared very loudly, so he was heard from far away.

Albee, Minda, and Bennie heard the commotion and swam swiftly to the surface.

"Oh, my goodness, where is Lukas going?" Albee asked a school of mackerel.

"Well, Lukas is moving to the Manila Zoo. He is so mean and menacing that boys and girls, moms and dads, and grandmas and grandpas, including us, were afraid of him. We're glad he is leaving and we will never miss him!" said one of the mackerels.

"Look at those pictures on that big boat: lions, tigers, and bears, oh my!" Minda exclaimed.

"Well, Lukas deserved to go somewhere. He will now have some new friends who probably have the same attitude as him. Maybe he will even love it there," said Bennie.

The local residents including Mr. Tambokon, the council members, and tourists were lining the beach and standing on the pier, happy to see the big boat hoisting Lukas. Finally, their wish was fulfilled.

With his last action of stubbornness, Lukas made his thrashing harder and his roaring louder.

Then the zoo veterinarian said to his assistant, "He is too much trouble. Let's put him to sleep right now!"

"Okay, sir, here comes the sleep gun."

He aimed, shot, and hit Lukas' belly, so in a few seconds the mean croc was sleeping like a baby. He snored and snored with his mouth wide open. The snoring was too loud and irritating, so the assistant grabbed a large, strong piece of tape and wound it around Lukas snout. Then there was silence all throughout!

Toot! Toot! The big boat announced that pretty soon it would start cruising. Humans and sea creatures were happy, because the mean and menacing croc was finally leaving!

"Hurrah! Hurrah! Bye, Lukas, and do not ever come back to Malapascua again!" yelled the inhabitants and tourists while waving.

Standing at the pier, Brad said, "Joan, Emily, and Ian, it's time to go back to Australia. Thank you, Albee, for helping Ian and good riddance, Lukas!"

"Yeah...Lukas, good you're gone. I like Albee. Can we come back next year, Dad?" asked Ian.

Emily added, "Of course, we're coming back, aren't we, Mom and Dad?" Jean and Brad responded with a smile.

Meanwhile Albee sighed, "Well, I hope that will be the last time we see Lukas."

"I feel bad for Lukas, but moving to the zoo might make him a good croc someday," said Minda.

CHAPTER FIFTEEN

The Gathering and Reunion

Meanwhile, the shark and fish species and other marine life were happy that Lukas, the mean croc, was gone. One day they decided to have a gathering and invited Albee, Minda, and Bennie.

A papa thresher spoke, "Albee, since you came back, those loud dynamite booms finally stopped. That was really very scary. Thank you for coming back, because you saved us from bad luck." All marine life nodded in agreement.

"Albee, Max and I will not bully and tease you again," said Rico. Then Max added, "And no bullying and teasing on Minda either!"

The young silvertip shark swam towards Albee. "If I hurt you before, I am truly sorry. I was too proud and haughty and I should not have behaved that way."

Bennie interrupted, "Do not bully and tease me either! You see, other crabs thought I did not belong with them, because I am too blue." There was some chuckling from the gathering. Then he added, "Here's what is true, getting rid of someone is no guarantee that something good will follow and that's exactly what happened to all of you. Any addition to this, Albee?"

"Well, teasing and bullying really hurts someone's feelings. May I say this…do not do to others, if you do not want others doing it to you. It's a very strong message. We may have different moms and dads, but we are all the same. We have the same needs, such as food for energy, clean water to swim in and drink, sleep to rest our bodies, and care from humans to make us healthy and happy. Last reminder, we should share and enjoy this large body of water. None of us own it. Thank you for welcoming us back and good luck to all."

Bennie whispered, "Albee, you sound very confident and no longer a scared shark—I'm very proud of you!"

"Thank you, Bennie. I owe everything to my parents."

"Now, I'm reminded of your mom and dad again! I'm upset."

"Bennie, if you want to be happy, look to the future, not the past. Just learn from the past, then build a better future."

"That's right, Bennie. Now, let's find something to eat. I am hungry," suggested Minda. With Bennie on Albee's back, they leaped up and then dove underwater.

Finally peace and happiness ruled Malapascua once again.

One day, Albee and Bennie took Minda to the area where the cave had collapsed hoping that

Sofia and Apo were able to come out. They swam around and had a hard time finding it. Then Albee spotted a familiar rock.

"Maybe it's somewhere near here. Ah! This must be it—I remember there was a large brown sharp rock sticking out at the side."

"Are you sure, Albee? Now there is an entrance to the cave, but you told me there were large rocks covering it," said Minda. Suddenly, about twenty large squid swam past them.

"This is it, Minda, and it is now open!" Albee looked around.

"Bennie, Bennie, come here."

Bennie, who was about to eat a live shrimp, let go of the shrimp to see what Albee wanted. He was somewhat upset, because he was hungry, but he swam quickly towards Albee and Minda.

"What, Albee? Oh…the cave is open! The cave is open! But where's your mom and dad?"

Then several divers came out of the cave and took photos of Albee, Minda, and Bennie. They waved, then swam away.

"It's open, but where did Mom and Dad go? Maybe they were long gone when the rocks were removed," said a sad Albee.

"I'm sorry to hear about what happened to your mom and dad," said a sympathetic Minda.

"Well, I was too dependent on them and I was so insecure. Their wish was for me to change. With them gone, I worked very hard so that I would become a smart, brave, wise, and strong thresher shark."

"You must be proud of what you have become, Albee," said Minda.

"Yes…I wished my mom and dad could see me now."

Suddenly, Albee heard a faint but a familiar voice that sounded like his mom. "Albee, Albee, where are you, son?"

Then another voice that sounded like his dad called, "Albee, are you around here? Can you hear me?"

"That must be the voice spirit of Mom and Dad coming from underneath that sand or maybe just my imagination," said Albee to Minda and Bennie.

"But I heard it too, Albee, so I do not think you are imagining it!" insisted Minda.

"I heard it too, Albee, and I usually do not imagine sounds," added quick-witted Bennie.

"So does this mean that my mom and dad are alive?"

Albee turned around and there he saw Apo and Sonia, gliding slowly with tails swaying from side to side.

"Mom and Dad! Where have you been? I missed you both and I thought I lost you forever!"

Albee rubbed his body against his mom and dad—sort of a thresher shark hug.

"Oh, Albee, it's a very long story, but to make a long story short, there were also divers that were inside the cave. The cave kept shaking every now and then and we were quite scared. Some rocks fell on your mom and me. After waiting for something to happen, someone brought a large boat with a long arm and removed those large rocks. They noticed that your mom and I and some trapped humans got hurt from the fallen rocks. We rode in a huge boat and they brought us to a very far place so that we could be strong again."

"And here we are. They just brought us back, so that we can be family again!" exclaimed Sonia. Then Sonia turned her attention to Bennie and Minda.

"So, you still have Bennie as your friend, Albee?"

"Yes, Mom, and I have another friend now too and her name is Minda. Her skin is creamy like mine, but she has some shading on her fins."

"Hello, Minda, nice to meet you." Minda moved her snout up and down—sort of shark sign that she was pleased with Sonia's friendliness.

"Glad to meet you too, Minda. We're happy that Albee now has a thresher shark friend," said Apo.

"Nice to meet both of you. Yes, I was surprised to run into Albee and Bennie in Torabeles Sea."

"Albee, did you go and visit your Uncle Baldo?"

"Yes, Dad, and sad to say, Uncle Baldo was hit by a fast running speedboat and did not make it."

"I feel sorry for my brother. Some of us will die from the careless hands of humans, and it should not be!" Apo looked sad and upset.

"But why did you go there?"

Bennie made a claw signal to Albee to allow him to explain.

"Well, after the cave collapsed, he thought that you were both dead. He missed you and he wanted to live with his Uncle Baldo because he was like a dad to him. Besides, he was bullied and teased in Malapascua. But everything is now fine and dandy. Albee is no longer worried that sea creatures will tease and bully. You are both alive and well! That is all that matters."

"Albee, you mean you are no longer being bullied and teased?" asked Sonia.

"Is it true, son?" inquired Apo.

"That is right, Mom and Dad. I am now friends with thresher sharks and all sea creatures. I will tell you all about what happened while you were gone, but not now."

"That sounds wonderful, Albee! Before…you did not have friends and now you have more than two friends. I told you that if you were patient, you would eventually have friends," reminded Apo.

"You are right, Dad, and I am glad that you and Mom are okay."

"Albee, I felt something different in you." Sonia swam near Albee, then poked his tummy with her right fin. "Are you really our son?"

"That tickles," he chuckled. "Mom, it's really me, your son, Albee—still albino, but wiser, smarter, and much braver now!"

"We are so proud of you, Albee…way to go, son," said Apo. Then he turned to face Minda.

"Minda, why did you decide to move to Malapascua?"

"Albee, Bennie, and I planned on working together to make humans change their bad behaviors so that we will all live in a safe and clean ocean. We do not know how…but maybe some good ideas will come someday." Then Albee and Minda intertwined the tip of their tails. Bennie hugged their tails with his largest claws—sort of a sea creature's sign of promising to work together!

"Sonia and I are very proud of you three!" They all beamed with happiness.

Then Bennie interrupted, "Excuse me, Albee…since you now have Minda as your shark friend and your mom and dad are back, I think it is time for me to go and find my own crab friends."

"Let's Work Together for a Clean and Better Ocean"

"Okay, Bennie, but please remember that you will always be my friend, even if you're a crab and thanks for your help. I will never forget you, bye my good friend! Please keep in touch."

"I will. Bye, Albee and Minda, it was a pleasure knowing both of you and I am very glad that Sofia and Apo are alive. Now I feel much better."

"That's okay, Bennie. We understand that you were just trying to help Albee," said Apo.

"That's right, Bennie, bye and good luck. Please be careful!" added Sonia.

"I will, and thank you, Apo and Sonia."

"Bye, Bennie...pleasure to know you and hope you will find a friend. We will be in touch," said Minda while waving her tail.

With those parting words, Bennie swam away slowly, passing two young manta rays and a family of sea turtles that said "Hi" to him and he answered back a weak "Hi."

Bennie decided to swim to a nearby coral reef to see if he could find something to eat. Suddenly, he spotted a female blue crab under a rock clinching a fish between her claws. Bennie swam faster.

"Wow! She is also very blue like me. She is just the right crab friend I am looking for!" Then Bennie noticed that she was munching on a dead mackerel. "Oh no! Can't she even find a better meal? That dead fish is disgusting! Argh...Argh! Yuck! Yucky! Very yucky! This lady crab needs some lessons in good eating!!"

THE END

Bennie

Seaweed Noodles

Jose

More about Albee,
His Home and Other Story Characters

MALAPASCUA (MALAPAS-KWA)

A tiny island located in the northern Pacific Ocean. This island is located closer to the equator, therefore, it is warm all year round. The weather and the clear blue water made it a perfect habitat for marine life including thresher sharks. It is situated in the Visayas Sea across a shallow strait from the northernmost tip of Cebu, Philippines. It is only about 1.6 miles long or an equivalent of 22.5 kilometers and 0.62 mile wide or about 1 kilometer.

The name "Malapascua" is said to be given by some Spaniards whose ship was stranded in the island on Christmas Day, December 25,1520, due to bad weather. Because they have to spend Christmas in an isolated island and away from their friends and families, the Spaniards called the island Mala Pascua, which literally means "Bad Easter." Presently, it has become a popular tourist attraction and a perfect destination dive for foreign and local divers because of the thresher sharks, bountiful marine life and the unspoiled underwater beauty. For island accommodation, there are comfortable hotels and motels for tourists and visitors. Local and western food are in the restaurant's menu. Therefore, if you do not like seafood you can order hamburger, hot dog, fries or pizza. You have to ride a Catamaran or "Bangka" to get to Malapascua Island. There are no passenger cars in the island but your feet could certainly give you some comfortable "rides" around! Bikes and motorcycles are the other options. -

(Source: M. K. Modina's Malapascua info collection).

THRESHER SHARKS *(Alopias pelagicus)*

Thresher sharks are a type of mackerel shark.

- Threshers grow to a length of 5 - 6 meters and about half is the huge scythe-like tail for which it is named. They have very small sharp teeth and very big eyes to see in the dark - 10 cm diameter in adults or about the size of a baseball. They like to eat squids, herring and mackerel and they use their tails to 'corral' the fish into denser schools to maximize their catch. The tail may also be used to stun fish via the whip-like strikes of their long tail. They stay in deep water during the day and move into surface waters at night to feed.

- Threshers can swim at high speed in short bursts and can completely jump high out of the water if threatened or provoked. They are not known to attack or eat humans but their long whip-like tails can hurt humans.

- Big eye threshers are ovoviviparous, meaning producing young from eggs hatched within the body. The unborn young thresher initially feed on the yolk sac and infertile eggs produced by the mother and mom usually bears two pups, rarely 5. Their gestation period or how long the baby threshers stay in the mom's tummy is 9 months. Therefore, they are similar to humans! The female thresher shark produces only 20 young threshers over her entire life. The maximum lifespan of male threshers is 19 years and 20 years for female.

(Source: M. K. Modina's Malapascua info collection)

SEA NOODLES or "LUKOT" to the Locals

The seaweed noodles are edible and they taste exactly like noodles but have some slight seawater taste to it. They are abundant in the Philippine region of Visayas and Mindanao.

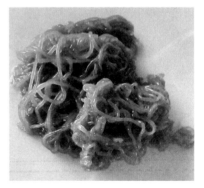

The local inhabitants would harvest these sea noodles and sell them in the local market. The noodles can be made into salads with vinegar, onions, ginger, pinch of salt and tomatoes - delicious. Another use is to enhance the flavor of fish stews - again delicious. There are factories in the Philippines that are commercializing seaweed noodles and processing them to make it look like pasta noodles. Seafood noodles can now be made into any dish that requires noodles and they are rich in calcium, magnesium and iodine.

(Source: M.K. Modina photo collection and E.Duran)

TOBLEE PLANT

This plant is commonly found in the Philippine island and can thrive in tropical climate. It looks innocent and would even look beautiful in someone's yard but they are deadly to the fish and other marine life. Illegal fishermen will extract the 'poison juice' from the stalk and spread it in the area where there are fish. The 'juice' will cut off the fish's oxygen supply and slowly kill the fish. It's a cruel and irresponsible way of fishing because it will kill fish that are not supposed to be harvested such as the baby, young and the pregnant fish. This is a bad use for this plant.

However, a toblee plant has some good use for humans too. For thousands of years local inhabitants have used this plant for medicinal purposes. They used the leaves and stalks to help relieve muscle aches and pains. Another use is to improve muscle tone. For those who cannot afford to see a doctor and buy medicines, this is their only choice. Hopefully, we can have this plant put to good use someday... perhaps treating some form of cancer and other deadly diseases.

(Sources: M. S. Otero photo collection and E. Duran)

WINGED-BOAT or "BANGKA"

Boat with winged-like extension on both sides for stability. For sun protection, a covered roof is usually installed. These boats are powered by motorboat engine. It can carry about 10 -20 passengers. This is one of the few means of sea transport when visiting Malapascua Island. (M. K. Modina Photo Collection)

OPEN CATAMARAN IN THE ISLAND OF CEBU.
MOSTLY USED TO HOP FROM ISLAND TO ISLAND.
(Source: M.K. Modina's collection)

Edna Duran is a Board Certified Nurse Practitioner in the state of Florida. She is currently employed at the C. W. Young VA Health Care System, Bay Pines Florida in the Endocrinology/Diabetes Department. Her love of writing started when she helped her eldest son John, then eight-years old, write a short story for their school writing contest. She was quite surprised that it won second place considering that it took them less than an hour to compose and make the illustrations for the story. The reason: John only told her an hour before he had to leave for school. Edna also holds a Bachelor's of Science degree in Elementary Education. She taught second grade students at a private school in Cebu City, Philippines. Her childhood dream of becoming a nurse was quite strong that she decided to leave the teaching profession and pursue a nursing degree. During the course of her professional nursing career she understood the importance of pursuing higher education. She completed her Master's of Science in Nursing at the University of Wisconsin, Milwaukee, Wisconsin. Still not tired of going to school, she enrolled for a post Master's Advanced Registered Nurse Practitioner (ARNP) course at the Uniformed Services University of Health Sciences in Bethesda, Maryland – distance learning. Having realized her dream in nursing, she decided to "revisit" the period when she used to teach second grade students by writing a story for children. Thus, *Albee a Thresher Shark* was born.

Hope Valiente lives in Cebu City, Philippines with his family. He presently works as senior graphic designer for a Cebu souvenir company designing t-shirts and merchandise for boutiques. His previous work experiences are storyboard and motion graphics artist for a Cebu Entertainment/Movie Production company, illustrator/artist for a Cebu Magazine and a TV station.

CPSIA information can be obtained
at www.ICGtesting.com
Printed in the USA
LVIC04n1140120615
441904LV00002B/1